Love, Sissela from
Great Nana
Marion

For Mary Harris Geddes
with love

SIMON & SCHUSTER BOOKS FOR YOUNG READERS
Simon & Schuster Building, Rockefeller Center, 1230 Avenue of the Americas,
New York, New York 10020, Copyright © 1992 by Heather S. Buchanan.
Originally published in Great Britain by Methuen Children's Books,
a division of Reed International Books Limited. First U.S. edition 1993.
SIMON & SCHUSTER BOOKS FOR YOUNG READERS is a trademark of Simon & Schuster.
Manufactured in Hong Kong
10 9 8 7 6 5 4 3 2 1
Library of Congress Cataloging-in-Publication Data
Buchanan. Heather S. This Little Piggy/by Heather S. Buchanan.   p.   cm.
Summary: A prose elaboration on the nursery rhyme "This Little
Piggy Went to Market," revealing what happened to him at the market
and how he came away again.
[1. Nursery rhymes—Adaptations.   2. Folklore.]   I. Title.
PZ8.1.B85Li   1993   [398.2]—dc20   [E] 92-11895 CIP
ISBN: 0-671-79351-9

This
Little Piggy

HEATHER S. BUCHANAN

SIMON & SCHUSTER BOOKS FOR YOUNG READERS
Published by Simon & Schuster
New York   London   Toronto   Sydney   Tokyo   Singapore

This little piggy went to market,
This little piggy stayed home,
This little piggy had roast beef,
This little piggy had none.
And this little piggy cried whee-whee-whee
All the way home!

There was once a little piggy who went to market all on his own; and this is why he went.

His poor father had tripped in a hole in the road, so he couldn't work at his job any more. He was a mailman and walked from house to house carrying all the letters and packages. For weeks he hadn't been able to earn any money and the Pig family couldn't afford to buy any food. There was nothing at all left in the house to eat.

Little Pig's mother did not know which way to
turn and his little sister walked around all day long
feeling sad. Everyone's tummy rumbled a great deal.
Four loudly rumbling tummies made a terribly
hungry noise.

One day, Little Pig decided that he must do
something to help.

Secretly he told his little sister his plan.

"I'm going down to the market to offer myself as a young working pig," he told her, "and I'll soon be able to bring back money to buy food for us all. Promise you won't tell. I want it to be a surprise for Mother and Father."

"I promise," she said, "but only if *you* promise to come back safely."

"Of *course* I will," he laughed, and he marched off down the road before he had time to change his mind.

The market was a long, long way from home, and it was some time before Little Pig came to the tall gates at the entrance.

A big farmer soon spotted him and scooped him up in his huge hands.

"Please sir," squeaked Little Pig, "I've come to find work."

"Have you indeed, my lad?" grinned the farmer. "And what work could a little pig like you do, I'd like to know? A nice bit of gravy and onions would go down well with you, little fellow, if you ask me."

With that he put him firmly in a pen behind all
the other enormous pigs, to await his turn to be sold.
While the farmers stood around, laughing at him,
Little Pig settled down patiently to wait, unaware of
the danger he was in.

    Meanwhile, Little Sister Pig went back indoors and found
her mother smiling because she had found an old potato with
roots growing out of it.
    Little Sister Pig wanted to eat it right away, but Mother and
Father Pig said they should plant it so that they could grow
even more potatoes.

Mother Pig took the big shovel and they all went outside.
It was hard work, but Mother Pig dug and dug until she
had made a deep hole. She asked Little Sister Pig to pass her
the potato.

Just then, she caught sight of something shiny deep down in the brown earth. She bent down and slowly brought out not one, not two, not just three, but *dozens* of gold and silver coins!

Father Pig and Little Sister Pig watched wide-eyed as the money piled up on the ground beside Mother Pig.

When at last she struggled to stand up, they gave a
whoop of delight.
"It must be our lucky day!" they cried.
"Let's eat!" shouted Mother Pig.
She gave Little Sister Pig a basket and sent her to buy
some food.
"Find your brother and tell him the news before you go,"
she said. "I can't imagine where he can be."

Little Sister Pig knew where he was, of course, but she didn't tell. "I'm sure he'll be back soon," she thought, and off she went.

First she went to the baker, because the Pig family had not eaten bread for many days.

Then she went to the grocer, because the Pig family had not eaten eggs for many weeks.

She ran to the vegetable stand next, because the Pig family had not tasted fresh, green brussel sprouts for more than a month.

Finally Little Sister Pig went to the butcher, because the Pig family could not even begin to remember when they had last eaten roast beef!

When Little Sister Pig arrived home with her overflowing basket, she was surprised to find that Little Pig still hadn't returned.

The cooking began. The beef roasted and the rolls toasted, but still he didn't appear.

When dinner was nearly ready Mother Pig said to Little Sister Pig, "Go and find your brother and tell him dinner's on the table!"

Little Sister Pig went to have one final look down the lane.
There was still no sign of Little Pig, so she decided that the
time had come to tell her parents what had happened.

She went back inside where they were sitting down to eat.
And then she said, in a very small voice, "I know a secret."

When Mr. and Mrs. Pig realized where
their little son had gone, and why he had gone,
and how long ago he had gone, they were horrified.

Father Pig put his crutch under his arm and Mother
Pig snatched up her hat and threw all the gold and silver
coins into her huge handbag.

She grabbed Little Sister Pig by the hand and set off
down the garden path at amazing speed, with Father Pig
hopping along behind them as best he could.

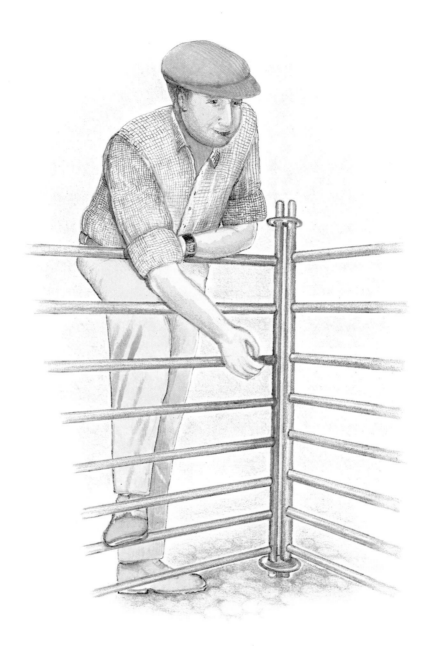

At the market, Mother Pig found her brave little son standing in a pen, looking very small indeed. The farmers were laughing as the auctioneer tried to start the bidding. Without losing another moment, Mother Pig rushed into the ring and threw down four gold coins from her bag.

"Please sir," she called to the auctioneer, "don't waste your time on this young pig. He is a very *bad* pig, a runaway pig and a truly troublesome pig. Let me buy him back and grow him into a nice fat *juicy* pig . . ."

And before the man had time to answer, she had pulled Little Pig through the bars of the pen and was running and running with him, with Little Sister Pig following as fast as she could.

When no one could see them, she stopped and kissed him. Her eyes filled with tears. Little Pig was of course very glad to see her, but his feelings were terribly hurt by the things she had said.

"Mother," he asked in a little puzzled voice, "why do you think I am such a bad pig?"

"Oh, my brave and beloved Little Pig," she cried, "they would not have given such a little pig *work* to do. They would have fattened you up and then they would have eaten you!" When she heard that, Little Sister Pig started to sob.

As they began to walk home, they met Father Pig hopping slowly toward them. He was very relieved to see his little son safe and sound, and delighted when Mother Pig rattled her handbag to show that she had plenty of money left for the Pigs' future.

Little Pig was happy, too. He led the
way, skipping around his family and shouting,
"Whee-whee-whee!" all the way home!